30

05

Lanca
Bowr
Prest
www.

D0184113

Mortimer's Picnic

Nick Ward

troika books

Lancashire Library Services	
30118132797600	
PETERS	JF
£6.99	27-May-2016
CRI	

Published by TROIKA BOOKS

First published 2016

10 9 8 7 6 5 4 3 2 1

Text and illustrations copyright © Nick Ward 2016

The moral rights of the author/ illustrator have been asserted

All rights reserved

A CIP catalogue record for this book is available from the British Library

ISBN 978-1-909991-27-9

Printed in Poland
Designed by Louise Millar, London

Troika Books
Well House, Green Lane, Ardleigh CO7 7PD, UK
www.troikabooks.com

For Austin William Penley

Mortimer was getting ready to go on a picnic with his best friend, Oggy. He had just finished packing his picnic hamper when a letter popped through his letterbox.

Sponge Cake

As well as the picnic,
Mortimer packed
some medicine,

a get well soon card,

and a storybook.

Then he set off for his friend's house.

"Oh, bother," said Mortimer,
putting up his umbrella as it started to rain.

Then – **WHOOSH!**
a strong gust of wind lifted
him up in the air . . .

and – **SPLASH!**
Mortimer landed in the
middle of a wide river.

"HELP!" he cried.
"I can't swim."

"GRRRNASH!"
growled a great big crocodile as he popped his head
above the water and sniffed the picnic hamper.
"I'll carry you across . . .

**if you give
me your
sausages."**

"But they're for my best friend," said Mortimer.

"I eat little rabbits too!" snarled the crocodile.

So, Mortimer gave the crocodile the sausages and . . .

SNAP! the crocodile gobbled them all up and took Mortimer to the other side of the river.

Mortimer was wet and very cold
but on he went into a dark and scary forest.
(The crocodile, who was still hungry,
crept along behind him.)

BEWARE
DARK
AND
SCARY
FOREST

The forest grew darker and scarier,
and soon Mortimer didn't know which way to turn.
"Oh help!" he cried with a shiver and a sniff.
"I'm lost." (The crocodile was lost too.)

"GRAARR!"
growled a fearsome wolf, leaping from
behind a tree and sniffing the picnic hamper.
**"I'll show you the way if you
give me your cake."**

"No!" said Mortimer.
"It's for my best friend, who's poorly . . .
Atishoo!"

"I eat little rabbits too!"
growled the wolf, snapping his sharp teeth.

So, Mortimer gave the wolf his cake.
The wolf gobbled it all up and led him through
the tangled trees to the edge of the forest.

Mortimer's nose was starting to run and his throat was feeling sore, but he carried on along a rocky road. (The wolf, who was still hungry, crept along behind him, and the crocodile tiptoed behind the wolf.)

Mortimer came to a rickety bridge.

"HALT!" ordered a hairy mountain troll, jumping out of a cave and sniffing the picnic hamper. **"You can't cross my bridge unless you give me your pumpkin pie."**

"No!" said Mortimer.

"It's for ...
Sniff!
my best friend."

But the mountain troll
snatched the hamper
and gobbled down
the pumpkin pie.

Yum, yum, yum!

"I'm still hungry," growled the troll, looking into the empty basket,

"And I eat little rabbits too!" He roared and he snarled and he chased Mortimer across the bridge.

"Come back!" I saw him before you howled the wolf.

"I saw him first!" snapped the crocodile.

And they all chased after Mortimer.

"We eat little rabbits!"

they roared.

Just then, a great big hand came down
from the sky and picked Mortimer up.
A giant ogre had grabbed him.

"RARR!"

bellowed the ogre and stamped
his massive feet.

"AND I EAT CROCODILES AND WOLVES AND HORRID HAIRY TROLLS!"

"Eeek!" squealed the troll,
the wolf and the crocodile.
And off they ran.

"Thank you, Oggy," said Mortimer.

"ATISHOO!"

"What are you doing here?" asked Oggy the giant ogre.

"I came to look after you," said Mortimer.
"I brought our picnic, but it's all gone.
I brought a get well soon card and a storybook,
but they're all soggy."

"Never mind.
I'm feeling better now," said Oggy.
"But **YOU** look dreadful.
You need looking after."

So Mortimer went back to Oggy's cave and was sent straight to bed with a giant hot water bottle.

"Thank you, Oggy," said Mortimer as the giant gave him a spoonful of medicine.

"Don't be silly," said Oggy, opening the soggy storybook.

"That's what best friends are for!"